Baked Beans

Written by Jane Wood

Contents

Where Do Baked Beans Come From?

Baked beans are made from **haricot** beans.

This field is full of haricot bean plants.

2

The beans grow in **pods** on the plants.

Beans need rain and sunshine to grow.

3

The beans are picked
when they are
dry and ripe.

The beans are taken
to the **factory**.
At the factory,
they will be made
into baked beans.

How Are Baked Beans Made?

First, the beans are sorted by size and color. Then they are washed.

Next, the beans are
soaked in hot water.
This makes them soft.

Then tomato
sauce is made.

Then the beans
are put into cans
and covered
in tomato sauce.

Next, the beans are **sealed** in the cans.

The cans are cooked and then cooled.

Finally, the baked beans are ready to go to the stores.

Eating Baked Beans

Baked beans are good for you.

They help you run fast

and work hard.

Meals with baked beans

Baked beans are very easy to cook.

You just heat them up.

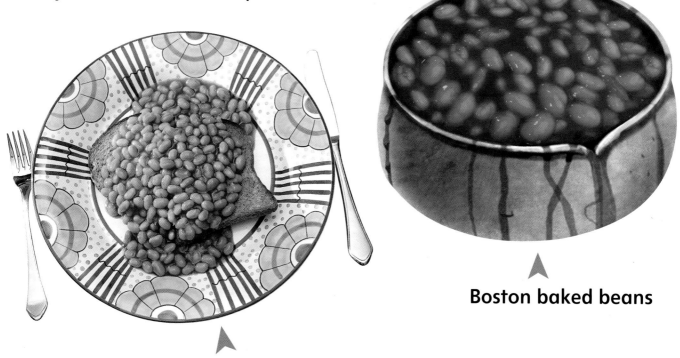

baked beans on toast

Boston baked beans

How to Grow Haricot Beans

1

In spring, plant the beans 2 inches deep.

2

Water them at least once a day.

3

Give the plants

some sticks to lean on.

They will soon get to the top.

4

The beans will be ready to eat in the summer.

Glossary

baked beans on toast - a way of eating baked beans in England

factory - a building where things are made

haricot - the kind of bean used to make baked beans

pods - a part of a plant where beans grow

sealed - closed so that air cannot get in

Index